Dear Parents and Educators,

Welcome to Penguin Young Readers! As parents and educators, you know that each child develops at his or her own pace—in terms of speech, critical thinking, and, of course, reading. Penguin Young Readers recognizes this fact. As a result, each Penguin Young Readers book is assigned a traditional easy-to-read level (1–4) as well as a Guided Reading Level (A–P). Both of these systems will help you choose the right book for your child. Please refer to the back of each book for specific leveling information. Penguin Young Readers features esteemed authors and illustrators, stories about favorite characters, fascinating nonfiction, and more!

Happy Easter, Tiny!

LEVEL **1**

GUIDED READING LEVEL **D**

This book is perfect for an **Emergent Reader** who:
- can read in a left-to-right and top-to-bottom progression;
- can recognize some beginning and ending letter sounds;
- can use picture clues to help tell the story; and
- can understand the basic plot and sequence of simple stories.

Here are some **activities** you can do during and after reading this book:
- Read the Pictures: Use the pictures to tell the story. Have the child go through the book, retelling the story just by looking at the pictures.
- Sight Words: Sight words are frequently used words that readers must know just by looking at them. They are known instantly, on sight. Knowing these words helps children develop into efficient readers. As you read the story, have the child point out the sight words below.

all	did	he	there	what
are	have	no	too	where

Remember, sharing the love of reading with a child is the best gift you can give!

—Sarah Fabiny, Editorial Director
  Penguin Young Readers program

*Penguin Young Readers are leveled by independent reviewers applying the standards developed by Irene Fountas and Gay Su Pinnell in *Matching Books to Readers: Using Leveled Books in Guided Reading*, Heinemann, 1999.

For M. & D., with continual gratitude—CM

To Cash Alexander Davis, my wonderful
grandson. I love you and I pray you will know
and love God with all you have.
You are a great blessing!—RD

PENGUIN YOUNG READERS
An Imprint of Penguin Random House LLC

Penguin supports copyright. Copyright fuels creativity, encourages diverse voices, promotes
free speech, and creates a vibrant culture. Thank you for buying an authorized edition of this book
and for complying with copyright laws by not reproducing, scanning, or distributing any part of it
in any form without permission. You are supporting writers and allowing Penguin to continue
to publish books for every reader.

The publisher does not have any control over and does not assume any responsibility
for author or third-party websites or their content.

Text copyright © 2018 by Cari Meister. Illustrations copyright © 2018 by Richard D. Davis.
Published by Penguin Young Readers, an imprint of Penguin Random House LLC, 345 Hudson Street,
New York, New York 10014. Manufactured in China.

Library of Congress Cataloging-in-Publication Data is available.

ISBN 9781524783853 (pbk)   10 9 8 7 6 5 4 3 2 1
ISBN 9781524783860 (hc)   10 9 8 7 6 5 4 3 2 1

Happy Easter, TiNY!

by Cari Meister
illustrated by Rich Davis

Penguin Young Readers
An Imprint of Penguin Random House

I love Easter!

Tiny does, too.

4

We color eggs.

6

It is time for the egg hunt.

Look at all the dogs!

Ready.

Set.

Go!

Tiny looks by the tree.

No egg.

Tiny looks by the bench.

No egg.

Tiny looks by the fence.

No egg.

The hunt is over.

There are no more eggs

to find.

Tiny is sad.

It is okay, Tiny.

We can have an egg hunt

at home.

Wait, Tiny!

Where are you going?

Tiny runs to a bush.

He barks and barks.

What is it, Tiny?

Did you find an egg?

Look!

It is the Easter Bunny!

Happy Easter, Tiny!